PUCKSTER'S CHRISTMAS HOCKEY TOURNAMENT

CANADA

FENN
TUNDRA

PUCKSTER

BY LORNA SCHULTZ NICHOLSON
ILLUSTRATED BY KELLY FINDLEY

Coloured lights sparkled against the night sky. Puckster slung his hockey bag over his shoulder and stared at them, a big smile on his face. This time of year was so magical. He and his pals had just finished their last practice of the year on the outdoor ice. Just three more sleeps before Christmas!

"I can't wait until Christmas!" Charlie bounced up and down. "This year we're all going to be together."

"Yeah, and at the best hockey tournament ever," said Manny, antlers wiggling.

"I've never stayed in a hotel room for Christmas," said Roly.

"It will be fun, but different to be away from home." Sarah stared up at the night stars.

"Christmas is magical everywhere in the world," said Francois. He paused. "Do you think Santa will come to our hotel rooms?"

"He has to," squeaked Charlie. "That's his job!"

This year *was* going to be different. Puckster and his pals were attending the IIHF World Junior Championship, and everyone was excited. Because he was the stick boy for Canada's National Junior Team, Puckster was leaving early on the big bus with the players. All of his pals and the team's families were coming the next day. They would be at the tournament for Christmas morning.

Puckster smiled and high-fived his friends. "I can't wait to give you your gifts."
Charlie jumped up and down. "What did you get me?"
"He's not supposed to tell." Manny laughed. "Christmas is about surprises."

After a long bus ride, Puckster and the players arrived at the arena. Big fluffy snowflakes landed on Puckster's head as he carried the sticks to the dressing room. The boys practised for two hours. Puckster got them water and towels. He watched, amazed, at how fast they could shoot and skate.

After the practice, when all of the equipment was put away, Puckster left the arena to go to his hotel room. Bigger snowflakes fell from the sky, and the snow was now knee-deep on the ground. Puckster tromped through the drifts to get to the bus.

The next morning, Puckster woke up in his strange hotel bed. He jumped up and pulled back the curtains. The snow was as high as his window—and it was still falling! Puckster put on his Hockey Canada sweatsuit and ran to breakfast.

The players and coaches were eating scrambled eggs and oatmeal, but no one was talking. They all looked sad.

"What's wrong?" Puckster asked.

One of the boys pointed his finger at a television, where a reporter was giving the weather report. "All the highways are closed because of the snow," he said.

"Oh no!" Puckster covered his face with his paws. "Our parents and friends won't be here for Christmas!"

That night was Christmas Eve, and Puckster and the players gathered for a festive dinner. Everyone was quiet as they ate their roast beef and mashed potatoes. Christmas music played in the background. A few of the boys tried to have fun and be jolly, but it was so hard.

When Puckster went to bed that night, he stared out his window at the hotel's Christmas lights. Somehow, they didn't look so magical here. It just wasn't Christmas without his family and friends. Tears fell from his eyes and landed on his fur. He wiped them away with his paw.

11 🍁

When Puckster woke on Christmas morning, he quickly looked around his room. Had Santa come? He searched under the bed and on the top of the television and in the closet for his presents. There were none. Puckster couldn't believe it. He sat back down on his bed and thought and thought. Then, he had an idea!

Maybe they were under the hotel Christmas tree! Puckster ran to the lobby.

Yes! There were *lots* of presents under the tree. He shook a few, sure that they were for him. But they weren't. They were fake—just empty boxes wrapped in pretty paper. Santa must not have been able to find Puckster so far from home. And far from his family and friends.

On the bus to the arena, all the players were quiet. Some listened to music. Others read. But no one said anything about Santa not coming. Puckster knew he had to do something.

When the boys were practising, Puckster snuck away from his spot on the bench. He found some white paper towels and shredded them to make a big white beard.

He went to the lost and found and searched through the plastic bin. He found a pair of glasses and a big pillow. He put the glasses on and shoved the pillow under his shirt. He dug deeper into the bin and yanked out a big black belt and some black boots.

When the boys came off the ice, dripping with sweat, Puckster was waiting.

"Ho ho ho," he said, rubbing his giant pillow tummy with his paws.

The boys just looked at him and laughed.

Puckster hung his head. His plan hadn't worked. No one believed he was Santa.

The team captain patted Puckster's shoulder. "Thanks for trying," he said, "but it's okay. We're here to play hockey. All we want for Christmas is a gold medal."

Puckster nodded. The captain was right. They were there to play hockey, and Puckster had a job to do. He had to be the stick boy and number one fan! He emptied all the water bottles and lined up all the sticks. Soon it was time to go to the bus.

This time, the snow was almost waist-deep. As Puckster and the team trudged across the parking lot, a strange sound drifted through the quiet winter air. Puckster stopped walking. What was it? He listened harder.

Ring, ring.

The noise got louder and louder.

Ring, ring.

Bells! It sounded like Christmas bells! And people singing Christmas songs.

Puckster stared down the road. Through the snow he saw a huge sleigh, pulled by reindeer. A man with a white beard and a red outfit and a big jolly belly sat in the front seat.

"It's Santa!" Puckster clapped his paws.

"It *is* Santa!" all the boys exclaimed.

Santa's sleigh was pulling another sleigh—and this one was even bigger. It slid easily across the snow, even though it was full of people. Puckster could see Charlie jumping up and down, and Manny's antlers moving. All the parents and friends waved and yelled, "Merry Christmas!"

"Ho ho ho," said Santa as his sleigh screeched to a halt. He stood and pulled out a long piece of paper. "Every boy on this team wrote me a letter asking for a gold medal for Christmas."

He winked at all the players. "You will have to work hard for this Christmas gift."

"Don't worry, Santa," they all replied, "we will!"

At the gold-medal game, Santa sat in the stands with all the other fans. He clapped and cheered and laughed big belly laughs, especially when Puckster danced.

When the buzzer finally sounded and Canada had won, Puckster high-fived Santa. The boys' Christmas wishes had all come true, and their friends and family were there to see them receive their gold medals.

It really was the best Christmas ever!

PUCKSTER'S TIPS:

Always believe that good things will happen.

Never give up on a goal or dream.

Family and friends are important in your life.

PUCKSTER'S HOCKEY TIP:

To be a good hockey player you must **always play your hardest**, no matter what the situation.

Good luck!